This book belongs
to the amazing:

....

For Toby, winner of the
National Literacy Trust's
'On The Shelf' auction

First published in Great Britain in 2019 by Hachette Children's Books

Copyright © Steve Antony 2019

Hodder Children's Books
An imprint of Hachette Children's Group
Part of Hodder and Stoughton
Carmelite House
50 Victoria Embankment
London, EC4Y 0DZ

HB ISBN 978 1 444 94470 9
PB ISBN 978 1 444 94471 6

Printed in China

An Hachette UK Company
www.hachette.co.uk

Hodder
Children's
Books

MIX
Paper from
responsible sources
FSC® C104740

AMAZING

Steve Antony

Some children have cats.
Some children have dogs.

I have a dragon.
His name is . . .

I taught Zibbo how to fly.

Zibbo taught me how to . . .

We do everything together, Zibbo and me . . .

We laugh.

We sing.

We learn.

We sail.

We dance.

We snack.

We draw.

We snooze.

And all my friends love Zibbo too.

We like to play basketball too.

He's not quite so good at that!

But, most of all, Zibbo and
I love going to parties.
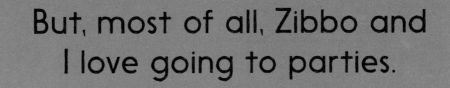

In fact, Zibbo loves parties so much . . .

he sometimes gets a little too . . .

Zibbo may be different,

but he is
MY BEST FRIEND.

When we're together . . .

I know that ANYTHING is possible.

Because Zibbo is . . . .

Just the way he is.

Also by Steve Antony:

Please Mr Panda

Steve Antony

I'll Wait, Mr Panda

Steve Antony

Thank You, Mr Panda

Steve Antony

Goodnight, Mr Panda

Steve Antony

'This picture book is hard to beat.' *The Times*

THE QUEEN'S HAT

'This picture book is hard to beat.' *The Times on The Queen's Hat*

THE QUEEN'S HANDBAG

Steve Antony

THE QUEEN'S PRESENT

Steve Antony

THE QUEEN'S LIFT-OFF

Steve Antony

Unplugged

Steve Antony

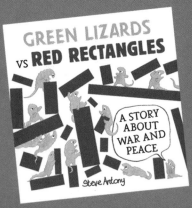

GREEN LIZARDS VS **RED RECTANGLES**

A STORY ABOUT WAR AND PEACE

Steve Antony